Psalm 86

BECOME WANTED ENTERTAINMENT
PRESENTS

A STORY BUILT ON JUSTICE, SEX, AND POWER

SEASON ONE

A Story Created by
DAVID GEARY

Editorial by
CESAR HINOJOSA

Written by
DEMETRIA COLEY

All rights reserved. No part of this book may be reproduced in any manner without written permission except in the case of brief quotations included in critical articles and reviews. For information, please contact the author.

Copyright © 2023 by
BECOME WANTED ENTERTAINMENT

Printed and Bound in the United States of America

All characters appearing in this work are fictitious.
Any resemblance to real persons, living or dead, is purely coincidental.

ISBN: 979-8-218-15965-8

Original Logo Design: David Geary
All artwork including photography, cover art, and the AMBROSIA logo Copyright © 2022 by
BECOME WANTED ENTERTAINMENT

BECOME WANTED ENTERTAINMENT
First Printing
www.becomewanted.com

ALICE TAMEEKA COLEY

AMBROSIA: SEASON ONE

Crawling under your nightstand back in Brooklyn, curiosity led me to your collection of Black novelists after watching how the pages kept you company through your literature journey. You introduced me to reading for an escape and unknowingly encouraged me to delve deeper and expand my imagination.

I followed you everywhere because you always provided the adventure I needed. Not to mention our warm walks with my sisters to the nearest library to uncover our next read; you were the best at so much.

From swapping books with you while I'm in town for a visit to shipping you your favorite interest to make up for special occasions, I take great joy in recreating what you did so well.

You birthed a writer, Mommy, and this one's for you.

Demetria

DANCER IN THE STREET

AMBROSIA: SEASON ONE

FREELAND PUBLIC HOUSING COMPLEX
WAILING NINYA PLACE
07:00 AM

"Fah-uck! We got another one for ya."

All is still this Thanksgiving morning, whereas grave stains of blood coating the street unveil various paired lights of caution and justice bouncing aimlessly throughout Freeland City's **Wailing Ninya Place**.

Swapping regard for how she died with *who* she once was, on-duty police officer, **Howie Liveright**, celebrates a body flooding the scene unworthy of his respect.

"Hurry up, will ya! We ain't got all day!" Deemed *too* dangerous to prosper, Ninya Public Housing is infamous for its crime-related activity, domestic violence, and gang brutality. In summary, Wailing Ninya Place is a street where it's wise to mind your business or your body will be the next tragedy to appear in the paper the following day.

DANCER IN THE STREET

"This is gross." Lingering over the bare necks of The Blue, a bone-chilling breeze invites them to pull the collars of their winter-issued jackets closer to their skin. Their assignment was to enclose the murder scene, and *that* they did. However, they've been suffering in the middle of wolf territory, shuffling their feet since 5AM.

"**Burkman**!" Marching through his unit, Officer Liveright steps off the sidewalk and into the street to join the department's lead homicide examiner. "Uh, our homicide hero is running behind, and I need this body out of the street ASAP!" he barks.

Living up to be the big, the tough, and the brave, Liveright's newbies sporting their untried badges could barely endure the scene before them. The shock from the spectacle had drawn them into an emotional solitude as they stood amongst one another like mutes, hoping to be relieved from their duty and sent home to their family sooner than later.

AMBROSIA: SEASON ONE

Embracing the pavement for the public to see, gore had oozed from her open wounds to cover her like a second skin. Furthermore, her injuries are unexplainable.

Flawed with the absence of discretion, Liveright approaches the medical operative and jabs him with a sharp elbow, insisting on immediate compliance. "We don't need another stripper uproar on our hands, do you understand?"

Destin Wesley Burkman, the precinct's overqualified Pathologist, acknowledges the snappy officer, and with his leather medical briefcase in hand, he joins him in the street. Meanwhile, when curiosity and tension knot between his eyebrows, he breathes when he recognizes *her*.

"Shit."

From the main street, creeping through a line of squad cars, a black 1976 Fastback hums quietly until its tires come to a rolling stop. The driver cannot be identified through

DANCER IN THE STREET

the windshield, yet the exhaust from its pipes leaves a trail of noiseless smoke to dance with the frigid atmosphere at its rear.

"This better be him."

VRMM...

Achieving the curb from the back of The Blue, the driver activates the vehicle's high beams to find Liveright, shielding his eyes from the uninvited, "Goddamn hotshot."

Moments after her arrival, she removes her keys from the ignition, swipes her badge from the dash, and steps out.

SLAM!

Her copper leather jacket fits perfectly. Her thighs are bound by midnight-blue denim and worn combat boots with thick buckles knocking against her ankles. Standing just above five feet, she is gorgeous, leggy, and snatched, compelling them all to stare as she nears the scene.

"Destin..." Hiding her hands in the back pockets of her jeans, her voice trembles with

AMBROSIA: SEASON ONE

false hope as she combs his face with her wide, brown almond eyes.

"Aren't you out of your jurisdiction, *ma'am*?" Answering before the Pathologist, Officer Liveright acts as a go-between and further inflicts rudeness. Correctly so, only those oK'd by the Lieutenant are permitted to scrub the scene. However, the stunning woman ignores him, allowing her firm resolve to propel him to stand down. "Ugh, carry on."

"Detective Howard, it's bad."

The uniforms surrounding them didn't want her there, and she felt that coming in. Nonetheless, Liveright requires them to clear a path for her and Destin, allowing them to bypass his threshold.

FLASH!

Standing firm before an arrangement of graphic evidence markers carefully placed along the stage, Howard appears numb, yet her eyes are wide open on this one.

DANCER IN THE STREET

"How?" Her voice is small under the weight of this finding. The sole article of clothing attached is a calf-length sequin boot designed with a translucent platform pinching $5's, $10's, and $20's.

Puzzled with that which is still unclear, Howard turns away while Destin continues to document the scene.

"Black female, adult, no identification." Holding back what can only be documented as anger, she recognizes his attempts to unravel the killing details and its terrifying riddles and follows him under the yellow tape.

FLASH!

"This is exactly how she was found." Gesturing his gloved hand towards the victim's chest, he leans in, tracing the wounds with his finger. "Three deep ones," he reveals, "… with multiple cuts along her ribs, genitals, and thighs."

FLASH!

AMBROSIA: SEASON ONE

"Her throat is overkill; wrongful for sure." Leading with empathy, he falls concerned with the policewoman scrutinized by an entire police unit behind her.

"Time of Death?" The woman's head rests just inches away, decapitated from her body, and despite the maiming of her temple, her lips are softly parted as if she had accepted her fate.

"I'd placed it no more than an hour ago." Next, he tucks his camera to prepare the scene for extraction. "I'll have to take her away for my studies." Numb to Destin's comments, worry reaches Howard while her male counterparts murmur in malice.

"Make sure she gets there safely, Des." Lingering longer than necessary, Howard locates her car and cuts through the weary police officers, slicing their nasty words as she struts by.

"I will," he warns.

"Alright, fellas, let's wrap up and get

DANCER IN THE STREET

this whore outta here!" Liveright announces.

SLAM!

She shut her car door with enough force to echo off the tall brown buildings encircling her; she is pissed. Instantly, she hurls her badge to squeeze the steering wheel until she tires out. Howard's had enough—enough with the missing, enough with the dead girls, and enough with **The Blue**. This is her breaking point.

BEAUTY PROVOKES

BEAUTY PROVOKES

GIBSON PRIME POLICE PRECINCT
HOMICIDE ADMINISTRATION
10:19 AM

Marching down the pale corridors of Homicide, a familiar police operative wearing a copper jacket, blue denim, and combat boots calls for the attention of her allies with each thunderous step, loud enough to draw them out.

"Here she comes…."

Scanning each police officer arranged along her course, she shudders at the mere glance of their fuzzy faces and debatable badges. After the chilling event of the murdered woman found earlier, she expected more from them.

Approaching a bend at Open Records, Detective Howard enters a respective office, hidden between the male's lavatory and the only freestanding water fountain in the entire department to discover—

AMBROSIA: SEASON ONE

"I want the case!" A nameplate positioned at the edge of *his* desk stacked with restricted cases, and a timeless 26oz whiskey decanter crafted from fine crystal reads **J. Claire Schillaci**: *Lieutenant of the Town*.

Aiming to squeeze the man-with-the-brass for the investigation, a magnific portrait of a senior police captain looms over her, reminding her of whom she is speaking. Even further, she is surrounded by framed class-act achievements signed off by the mighty city officials appointed over her.

"What you want, Howard is none of my concern. And leave the door open…my boys would like to hear what you have to say." There is no such thing as privacy in his ward; besides, with the sum of fifteen years of service glued to his collar, perhaps he's heard it all.

"Lieutenant, with due respect, I'm the one you would want on this case," she states. But, no secret to her, this Lieutenant's nasty habits

BEAUTY PROVOKES

have managed to leak through his shield, and as their dialogue begins to unravel, whispers about the dead woman invade his chamber.

"Nobody wants to touch that case."

"She is the seventh dancer found in under two months, Lieutenant," she swears. Lacking a convincing report in full, she stands before him, deeply bothered, with her arms crossed tightly under her full breasts. She wants this case, and he can feel it.

Moments in, the stout Lieutenant rests his paperwork to discover her ideal eyes roaring at him beyond her dusty-blonde afro for a mane, only to satisfy his condescending ways.

"Whores." The word nearly snaps Howard in two, "You meant 'whores,' correct?" Her rich skin lusters with intense displeasure. This man has barely any empathy to share, as she is reminded daily. "Perhaps she was the worst finding at Ninya Place, but a dead stripper isn't worth this department's time or resources. Haven't you figured this out

AMBROSIA: SEASON ONE

by now?"

"Lieutenant, a murder is still a murder, and more are happening with no tact in a community fertile with young women." She goes on to stand her ground until—

"You don't get it." He then flings a photo from the killing onto the start of his desk for her to see. "What were you doing at my crime scene, Howard? You're Missing Persons." Moving to cut her short, Schillaci releases a burst of laughter that offends before going on, "I should suspend you."

His words fail to stun her. Constantly scrutinized as the only black woman to operate under **Gibson Prime**, their efforts have only hardened her, preparing her for a moment when she wins, and perhaps now is that moment.

"We've seen some messy stuff out there, and I mean some real violence, Lieutenant. But what we found this morning is the work of someone who isn't afraid of you and surely doesn't give a fuck about this division."

BEAUTY PROVOKES

Following him with her eyes, she finally goes to insert herself where she believes is only inevitable, "Let me have this case, and *I'll* make you look good," she says. Quietly, the man's inner thinking can be told by each finger tap and eye squinted, and after having heard enough, Schillaci pushes away from his command table and takes to his feet.

"Dammit, Howard, those girls are lost!" Far too startled to respond, she stands appalled while outrage takes its form. "Screaming to leave daddy's house to do drugs and dance for a few lousy bucks! Who's really to blame here, huh?" Perhaps the Lieutenant had seen more than one man could handle, and it's showing, "They know the risks of that damn club!"

Growing warm under her jacket, she can sense her body's thermos rise, bringing the vile from her stomach to reach the ridge of her throat, and although she can't explain it, she can finally feel the woman's suffering as if she were stuffed in the body bag with her.

AMBROSIA: SEASON ONE

SLAM!

"Give me clearance, **Jon**, or I walk." Suddenly, Howard is overtaken by a piercing noise in her ear, following the deadened voice of the Lieutenant.

"I will not send another agent to investigate some inappropriate…."

Entering a strange expanse outside their debate, Howard absorbs what's left of their public exchange and prepares her legs for combat, following an explosive tongue.

"HI-YA!"

Targeting Jon, Detective Howard raises her left knee to her chest and launches a karate kick into the edge of the heavy wood table.

SMASH!

Her hamstrings compress as the impact causes the workstation to shift, forcing Schillaci out of his chair.

"Howard, wait!" he shout. Then, to drive her point, the legendary portrait behind him falls from the wall to finish the frightened

BEAUTY PROVOKES

officer.

"Look here, you pathetic bastard!" Perhaps this isn't Howard, but allow the furious policewoman to tell it; it feels damn good, "If you think I'm going to support your incompetence, you have lost both your mind and your best investigator."

"B-Bobbi?"

Reflecting on her past words, Bobbi looks down to find her badge and firearm exposed, for she had just slammed the last six years of her career onto his desk. Nonetheless, she entered his ward to achieve one thing and one thing only.

"The case, Jon."

Lieutenant Jon Schillaci's lips begin to curl as he finds his seat, and as for Bobbi, she notices his favorable hand fall below the desk.

"Watch yourself, Detective…your sudden ultimatum is turning me on." Following each bend of her body with sweeping desire, his motives have led him far away from his

AMBROSIA: SEASON ONE

oath. Therefore: "You know Howard, colored women usually don't hold my attention, but uh…I'm willing to make an exception." Schillaci then locates the center of his desk where his hands finally join, permitting Bobbi to speculate what a man of his nature may have in mind, "How bad do you want this case?" Boom, it slips.

Bobbi's best access to exact justice has now been reduced to a sexual favor. How can she win this case without giving in to him? Lastly, while avoiding hostility, she abandons her badge, pivots carefully, and prepares for the exit; she can't.

"Go fuck yourself, Jon."

#

Later, at Wailing Ninya Place, Detective Bobbi Howard seeks seclusion behind the wheel of her Fastback across from the crime scene where the dancer was found.

BEAUTY PROVOKES

Her sights are fixed, focused on the very spot where the blood has stained the street.

Dangling her wrist out the roll-down window, she takes a deep drag from a burning Virginia Slim to ease her mind of anger and disgust and to think: it used to be that men would needle women who smoked in public.

"Bobbi, you've come a long way, baby."

A grueling hour and forty-two minutes had passed since she fled the precinct; she couldn't linger there much longer. The mere thought of Lieutenant Schillaci disturbed her to no end. The nerve; not another woman could have handled that situation the way she did, and while her imagination begins to race, she suddenly remembers to pay a particular ally a visit.

Casting a deep sigh, she flicks her cigarette, buries her most profound beliefs, and readies her vehicle to pull away from the picture.

GIBSON PRIME PRECINCT

75th

Date: October 13, 1976

Driven by resentment, power, and lust, Jon has grown into a rugged, unrelenting police officer. After his father's sudden retirement, Jon was promoted by his successor to Lieutenant, thus, steering Gibson Prime, Freeland's 75th precinct, to several victories.

However, his rising influence took a tragic turn while investigating a criminal bombing that took his arm and the last of Freeland's great defenders, excluding the legendary detective: Michael Gibson.

While many in Freeland have forgotten the city's brave heroes, Jon hasn't. Hence, he has evolved, now known for his no-nonsense mindset, an artificial Lance for an arm, and topmost desire to lead his division.

Sergeant Howie Liveright

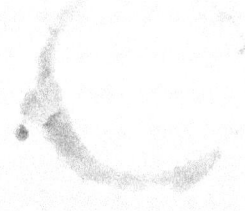

THE SILENT TRUTH

THE SILENT TRUTH

**GIBSON PRIME POLICE PRECINCT
DR. BURKMAN'S LABORATORY
12:42 PM**

"Fuck this…"

Tears begin to pool, threatening to burst as she fights the urge to snatch the label from a cold, stiff toe. Eyeing the tag marked with a ballpoint ink pen, she carefully rotates it to read: *dancer in the street.*

The room possesses an eerie chilliness to suit the tragic situation. Stainless steel cabinets and storage units surrounding the lab glint under the fluorescent lights beaming from above. Everything seems pushed away to provide space for an autopsy arranged in the center of the laboratory.

Staring at the white cloth and into the woman's face, Detective Bobbi Howard goes to remove it when—

"I didn't want to start without you."
Her hands immediately find their way into

AMBROSIA: SEASON ONE

her back pockets as the Pathologist enters the picture, "How are you coming along?" he asks. Making time for him was difficult. However, Howard hoped that he had concluded the examination.

"What do we know so far?"

Stumped for words, Destin discloses what little he has.

"Bobbi...I just don't get it." Since the morning, his findings have grown more and more disturbing, and while the atrocity thickens, so does Howard's curiosity. "I've conducted several postmortem examinations to discover causes of death and the extent of disease, but this?" he admits.

"What are you saying?" Discerning her detachment, Destin locates a pair of latex gloves from his lab coat and slips them on.

"Let me show you." He's a careful man, and under this unique condition, he is extra careful. "What I'm about to explain will scare you because it scared me too."

THE SILENT TRUTH

Starting from the top with both hands, he pinches at the corners of the dense fabric and gently folds it over.

"Damn." Suddenly, a look fixed with profound horror takes her beyond their discovery of the dancer in the street. Observing Bobbi from across the body, Destin, warm and mindful, continues.

"I have yet to complete my full analysis, but I did discover multiple fractures to the chest and ribs." Fixing his hands to demonstrate, Destin locates various color-filled marks indicating trauma. "Here and here, appear more consistent than her other injuries." The Pathologist, steering to prevail, hesitates as he carefully proceeds to reset the dancer's severed head.

Standing in utter silence, Bobbi seeks calmness once her watery eyes have been cleared of sorrowful tears. Noticing this, Destin steps away to allow his guest to study the fallen dancer alone.

AMBROSIA: SEASON ONE

"Who did this to you?" she whispers.

Beginning with her edged fingers, the Detective carefully trails her rigid wrist and arm, and as she circles the body, she eventually finds herself in this woman.

"I had to search her birth name." Once again, she shuttered, only to realize that she was lost for a duration. "Are you ready for this?" Bobbi knows only confidence in Destin; she trusts him, and although the two share history beyond the lab, she believes he is the only one who can help her.

"Yes."

Approaching the scenario with devotion to the practice, he opens his medical binder to locate the Howard Family, where he will announce their names as they appear on his list:

- Father: Julius Omarious Howard
- Mother: Evelyn Denise Howard
- Brother: Mosses Garrett Howard

"And **Blake**—"

THE SILENT TRUTH

"She had just turned twenty-six."

Her gaze intensified, and her jaw tightened when the truth finally dawned on her; she hadn't spoken to her in years. Bobbi's career had pulled her away from her family, and Blake's lifestyle could have smeared the shield she had worked so hard for. There are some things you can hide, but at what cost?

"The streets have been talking," Destin discloses. Peeling off his gloves, he confirms yet another opportunity that may work to the Detective's benefit, "A major performance occurred at **Diamond's** last night, and she was there."

Detective Howard, generally known to possess the righteous answer achieved by a staunch play-by-play process, remained still, provoked by the new information provided by the generous Pathologist.

"Alright."

She's aware of the glorified nightclub located beyond the bridge at Crown Heights

AMBROSIA: SEASON ONE

Terrace and the reality that her sister's killer is still on the loose; perhaps the two are enough to form a now convincing report.

"I need that clearance."

PLEAD WITH YOUR BODY

AMBROSIA: SEASON ONE

GIBSON PRIME POLICE PRECINCT
SCHILLACI'S WARD
05:50 PM

It has been a tedious day for Freeland's powerful police union, and while most have gone home, others are planning to call it quits, except Bobbi.

Highly regarded among further trades in both public and private sectors, The Blue mirrors a conventional proneness under the city's most dangerous circumstances. Meanwhile, as their membership rises, they have ultimately failed their most significant policewoman.

Like a helpless swan waiting for the wild to snatch her away, she stands anxiously near closed blinds, feeling foolish nonetheless.

"No matter how far you go, when it really counts, all they want is *this*." She shuts her eyes and swallows while her nerves extend upward from her belly to choke her. "You better make this your best…damn…lay."

PLEAD WITH YOUR BODY

The light penetrating the office reveals the oil painting, his winter coat draped over his sturdy armchair, and the timeless vessel, accentuating the rich hues of his favorite whiskey resting at the firm edge of his desk.

The doorknob jiggles before the barrier swings open as he enters, engaged in records held close to his face. His weighted footsteps tell his hefty physical frame while he shuffles along the wooden deck beneath him.

"WUH-HACK!" A nasty cough like that may indicate an illness expanding and, possibly, terminal. Then, realizing he is not the only one in the room, he carefully acknowledges the hidden Detective, following another aching cough.

"Sounds to me like you're a bit parched, Lieutenant?" She speaks from the dark overspread in his ward, observing his faulty arm concealed beneath his left shirt sleeve.

"And perhaps you have made the right decision in coming here, Howard." His voice

AMBROSIA: SEASON ONE

bleeds arrogance, to say the least, and yet, she moves in as he watches lustfully behind his tempted, blue-fixed regard. "Still laboring behind that dead girl?"

Seemingly relaxed, Bobbi sets her eyes upon him, drawing intrigue with each step she takes. She wasn't the same woman previously torn from his office hours ago; beyond this point, she is convinced. Unzipping her leather jacket to remove it, the risky policewoman flings it toward his suit coat to further draw his interest. Then, tugging at her shirt tucked below the waistband of her jeans, she raises the fabric over her head, baring her simple black undergarment to cover her most intimate region.

"I need that case, Jon," she confesses.

"How bad, Detective?" Schillaci can't help his greedy hands as he pulls her frame into his with an uncharismatic force. His early erection bulges against his slacks while its heat burns against the skin on her abdomen.

PLEAD WITH YOUR BODY

Just as a man with no finesse…she imagines, "Real bad." She then dislodges his hands from her; it's her call and not his—no longer the swan waiting to be snatched.

"You know I like my coffee black, Bobbi." Luring him away from his reports, she presses the Lieutenant toward his desk and chair. "Easy, Detective." Eager for what comes next, he caves to his finest operative and succumbs to her seductive assertiveness.

"Sit down." Getting acquainted with Jon like this is breaking her apart. She still remembers the good old days when she respected the brass—when she once admired him. Regardless, she came to persuade him, get the horny policeman to obey and cough up the case, and to do that, she must get him off first. "Can you relax for me, Jon?"

Kneeling in front of him, she reaches for his leather belt and dives straight into his trousers and beneath his boxers to reveal his pudgy member throbbing actively between

AMBROSIA: SEASON ONE

his legs.

"I've never had black pussy before," he speaks.

"Shut up."

Jon unravels. His belt, slacks, and undies have reached the floor. Peeking down at her, the Lieutenant discovers the policewoman stroking his penis with her hands while she kisses it; she's good. Entangled with lust, he can't pull away from her pouty lips fastened around it. She has him.

"That's it," he says. His words are activating. Thus, Bobbi makes her way down his shaft with a loose tongue, locking her lips around the pulsating tip. She honors Schillaci before plunging again, taking him to the back of her throat, where she leaves him. "Don't stop, you dirty slut." Sliding up slowly, she bobs her head one last time until he jerks, and in one spurt, he finishes, shooting hotly into her mouth.

"Time's up."

PLEAD WITH YOUR BODY

"AWWW!"

Moments have passed, and he's out like a light; she knew it wouldn't take long. Considering what she has done, Bobbi is sickened. Oral sex isn't even her edge. Even further, she didn't plan on giving her superior the honor of releasing anywhere on her body. But she had to secure the case somehow.

Resting on her knees, she shifts away to spit what is left of the Lieutenant onto the office-interlocked carpet, and when she returns, her ensuing intuitions lead to Jon's father's portrait darting down at them. He was watching the entire affair.

Slipping away quietly, she uncovers her badge and gun, still docked on Schillaci's command, exposed by his nameplate emitting rays by the moonlight.

Having won her sister's case, she goes for his desk to recover her essentials and returns to duty not before,

"You don't deserve this pussy, Jon."

GO HOME BOBBI

GO HOME BOBBI

CENTRAL FREELAND
BROWNSTONE LIVING
8:01 PM

Shutting the glove compartment with her badge inside, she holsters her weapon and lets herself out to welcome the frigid winds. With loss, guilt, and acceptance weighing on her shoulders, she stands in the freezing conditions unaffected and presses onward toward a typical brick structure of many rows and several windows.

Entering *Brownstone Living*, an inexpensive townhouse tucked away within Central Freeland, Bobbi closes the door behind her, fastens it, and starts up the limited staircase.

Passing through the public space, vivid beats of she and her Lieutenant invade her beliefs and then—

"Ugh." The thought of their inappropriate encounter had driven her to gag, "Only if there were another way."

AMBROSIA: SEASON ONE

Keying the lock to **3D**, horrific images of Blake's body stretched across the pavement, nearly decapitated, transmit stabbing pangs through her heart and gut. Thus, she commits to the twist of her key and goes in.

Peeling her coffee-brown jacket from her clammy shoulders, she drapes it over a chair in her living area, where she begins to pace before a vast lookout near a desk and television, a perfect platform bed, and a bookcase overflowing with paperbacks and various loose articles.

Sicken with guilt, she swipes the only photograph of her and her sister and ponders. Had she been more attentive, Blake might have sought her big sister instead of Ninya Place. Therefore, the intimate sentiment she has been holding back streams down her face.

She's broken.

MAKE A WISH

AMBROSIA: SEASON ONE

OLD FREELAND
SUNNYSIDE HEIGHTS
12:02 PM

"Time for cake!"

Seated giggles and rich smiles encircle a small dining table in a kitchen, where Evelyn arrives with a homemade chocolate cake just in time for a grand celebration.

Evelyn's apartment is an old thing. Her living room is graced with minor flourishes, an undersized television box, and an orange velvet Everly sofa large enough to fit three. School certificates and kindergarten photos of two beautiful girls adorn the limited hallway to her bedroom, where she and her daughters sleep in such a small living space.

Sprinting into the kitchen, the birthday girl stops in awe to find balloons, friends in party hats, colorful streamers, and a wide banner stretching across the archway that spells—

MAKE A WISH

"Happy birthday, Blake!"

Now that their superstar has arrived, Evelyn and the kids begin to sing. Jumping and cheering, they honor her turning seven.

"It's time to cut the cake!" Evelyn did her best to shower her youngest daughter with all she could afford. However, there were no candles to blow out this year. "Make a wish."

Then, with her eyes tightly closed, Blake pushes out the noise around her to pull her big sister close.

"What did you wish for?"

Smiling sweetly, she squeezes Bobbi and opens her eyes to honor their mother.

"For us all to stay together."

SUMMARIZATION
Fear him! Dr. Noir rules the dark underworld of Freeland City, haunting both heroes and villains with his uncanny ability to invoke fear and it has been too long since he has drawn blood.

HUSH-HUSH
Thought to have fallen at the hands of his arch-nemesis, Danny Black, we were wrong. He is very much alive and at large, for his bloodstained legacy lives on.

DEFENSE
While Dr. Noir lacks firearm expertise, his experienced mastership in mental disorders and lethal toxins, makes him more grounded than any other murderer in Freeland.

SUMMARIZATION
Bound by sacrifice and service to watch Freeland City, the man who refers to himself simply as Jon leads the Blue under the title *Lieutenant of the Town*. Yet, once regarded as one of the most mighty allies to ever lead, Jon was a proud warrior until sin ultimately became him.

HUSH-HUSH
Lieutenant of the Town originates from Jon's fine years as an active guardian of Freeland City alongside the legendary Michael Gibson, father of Marcus Gibson.

DEFENSE
His destructive Lance, which he calls it, is an intelligent prosthesis device equipped with many functions, most notably, a weighty concealed firearm.

SUMMARIZATION

Detective Bobbi Howard of Missing Persons has been many things: a defender, a rescuer, a liberator, and now, a victim of loss; her sister Blake. Thought to have escaped her family battle, Bobbi, now outraged, has accepted the case provided by Lieutenant Schillaci to punish the person behind her sister's murder.

HUSH-HUSH

Behind Freeland's tragic loss of their legendary Detective, Michael Gibson, Bobbi chose Gibson Prime as her primary command.

DEFENSE

Sally-Mae—Bobbi's mighty .38 Special has saved her on many accounts and is her soundest weapon to challenge the criminalities that prey on the lives she had sworn to protect.

IT'S A FAMILY MATTER

IT'S A FAMILY MATTER

ALTAR OF LOSS FUNERAL HOME
HILLTOP MEMORIAL
03:42 PM

Outside Alter of Loss, two wide doors swing open, with six young men, followed by a gathering of mourners, as they bear a mahogany-stained casket down a short flight of steps leading to the icy Avenue of Hilltop. Around here, low spirits always arrive on the second of December.

Shrouded in shame, they watch on with their lips pursed tightly. Not one tear for Blake is in sight. Hence, they linger only for a moment before moving on to battle the whistling chill.

Starting at the assembly's entrance, the town's bishop, wearing an ample funeral vestment, emerges to usher a middle-aged woman down the vertical gap. Her feet are unsure, and her head is heavy with sorrow; thus, they are careful in taking small steps

AMBROSIA: SEASON ONE

to safety. Furthermore, the continuous tremble in her shoulders proves obvious; she is devastated. As for the bishop, he attempts to console her before sending her off with her daughter's body.

Watching across from the remembrance, Bobbi oversees Evelyn in her private vehicle, following Blake's casket safely set in the funeral coach. The Detective was not invited, and why would they? Distance between them was established years ago, and yet—

"Wait."

Their mother stops the driver and looks beyond to find her oldest, making it up the hill. It's hard not speaking, and while Bobbi walks, Evelyn's dreams of a perfect family are drifting away too. Perhaps, she will never look back after this day just the same. Her youngest is off to be buried; meanwhile, her firstborn accepts the dangers of being a policewoman sworn to protect Freeland City.

Reaching the peak of Hilltop Park, Bobbi

IT'S A FAMILY MATTER

observes the services recession by way of her mother, pursued by multiple vehicles closely behind as they guide Blake to her final resting place.

"You're name wasn't on the program." Climbing the grassy ridge, the bishop finds the Detective seeking evenness behind Hilltop's Rock: a wide shallow-rooted sugar maple tree developed to endure the city's severe weather along with its most challenging moments.

"I'm not bothered by it. Besides, I'm working," Bobbi claims.

"Ah. It all makes sense now," ends the bishop.

SOME STRIPPER BITCH

SOME STRIPPER BITCH

MOUTH SERVICE EATERY
600 6TH AVE. SOUTH FREELAND
11:32 PM

"Where's my order for table ten?"

Amoy, the diner's youngest waitress, scurries around a small window to the restaurant's corner kitchen area, grabbing napkins and utensils before snatching up a hot plate of jerk chicken soaked in red sauce over a bed of yellow rice.

DING!

"Order up!"

Celebrated throughout Freeland, Mouth Service is recognized for the kitchen staff's hard work, spicy entrees, and unwavering commitment to feeding the homeless on the weekends and even the holidays.

Hidden privately in a booth in the back, Destin witnesses Bobbi as she enters the premises. Her full blonde afro bounces softly around her beautiful face, persuading him to

AMBROSIA: SEASON ONE

tidy his attire. Meanwhile, the collar around his neck tightens as he focuses on her as she nears. The dark denim bell bottoms stretch across her thighs like a second skin, pressing the Pathologist to take notice before she slides in at his table.

"Hey," she greets. Loosening her jacket at the top, the tempting peak of her breasts, well within view, invites him to react.

"Bobbi…" Following her feminine quirks, he communicates his capacity for her while his honest presence permits her to breathe eventually. "Glad you could make it." His warm wind drew her close; however, laboring through concerns of her own along with the closing of Blake's funeral, she did not come to chat casually.

"This is the only place open at this time of night." Understanding his weariness, she quickly learns this scene isn't his type.

"It's fine," he replies. Perhaps Destin is out of his element; 6th Avenue is classified

SOME STRIPPER BITCH

as the most dangerous area outside their jurisdiction.

"Good, I'm starving." She couldn't eat if her life depended on it; stress and worry had her stomach wrenched for days. Nonetheless, she's been waiting to speak with him since becoming Lead Detective on the case.

"So…Schillaci gave you the case?" At the mention of her captain, Bobbi's defense goes up, and his praise falls on deaf ears.

"No. I earned this case." The stiffness in her voice shocks the Pathologist. Since her encounter with Schillaci, she has been angry with herself. And now, sitting with Destin, she fights to remain moral in the presence of his underlying feelings for her. Delving deeper, how much is she accomplishing if she continues to give in—her body, her time? She cannot allow Destin to know, not now. She needs him on her side entirely. "So, what'd you got for me?"

While the night burns, an unnatural draft

AMBROSIA: SEASON ONE

summons the appetite of the streets, and while the two pursue a chase of her own, Bobbi begins to take in the diner's occupants with suspicion.

Sensing this, Destin adjusts his reading specs and leans in, releasing a deep sigh as he draws forward. He'd hoped they'd be able to share a decent meal that didn't accompany the horrors of his occupation.

"The details surrounding Blake's murder have reached The Board, and they want me to keep this as quiet as possible."

"So what are you saying, exactly?" Tension begins to surface while Destin continues to bear threatening information.

"They're trying to rule Homicide out."

DING!

"Order up!"

Instantly, Bobbi turns to set her eyes on Amoy, hoisting steamy plates of Brown Stew Snapper, Jerk Tilapia, and the house special: Oxtail Shrimp and Roti Skin.

SOME STRIPPER BITCH

To Bobbi's surprise, she makes her way to the front entrance to locate a couple of girls merely in their adolescence occupying another booth, wearing frayed shorts just over their fishnet pantyhoses to conceal their naive shortcomings. Ironically, exercising more confidence than their guiltless bodies can hold, their radiant smiles grace the entire diner with positivity and childish vibrancy.

"So…" Drawing Destin in with her soft upper body made pronounced under her oval-shaped expression, doubled-up lips, and full afro, an endless beat comes between them, dead to the rest of the surroundings. "What don't they want you to report?"

"It's more, I'm afraid." Believing he had pursued every angle surrounding Blake's study, a fretful cloud intrudes their booth, looming pain and puzzlement. Destin's conclusions have been eating at her core, constantly causing her to become troubled.

AMBROSIA: SEASON ONE

Hence, Bobbi's frustration ultimately reaches its peak.

"Oh, for goodness sake, Des. Who's jamming us?" Unbeknownst to Bobbi, her assumptions lead to somebody—when it is the other way around.

"I did a rape kit." Thunderstruck, Bobbi, impaired instantly, sinks into the burgundy cushion, for his words are both upsetting and unassuming. Thus, he has once again pierced the Detective. Regrettably, this emotional discomfort transcends her to destructive heights.

"What did you just say?" she begs.

Entering Mouth Service, a man of leverage, blessed with a textured crown formed to perfection, whips in, giving way to hanging bells above the entrance to ring obnoxiously throughout the eatery. His lustrous jewels draped over his attire have been custom-cut to serve his slick persona; the man's brilliance reveals his natural prerogatives.

"If something is there, Bobbi, and when

SOME STRIPPER BITCH

the test results come back true, you may have a potential witness."

DING!

"What the fuck are you doing in here?" Violence brews as the diner immediately surrenders to the dark man's vulgar mouthpiece. "You, get up." Abruptly, three of the four girls abandon the booth leaving one behind.

Digging for her driver's gloves, Bobbi cuts her eyes to find Amoy and the staff hiding behind the register and slides her left boot out and into the aisle, leaving Destin to ponder her intentions.

SHINK!

"Bitch, c'mere!" Next, his switchblade reaches his property, marking her face wet with fear. Observing from afar, the Pathologist takes notice. He's frozen. His palms are face down on the table, anchored with uneasiness, and his shoes are grounded due to the intense commotion at play. "You think you can hide from me?" Then, with a lift of his blade, his

AMBROSIA: SEASON ONE

wrist becomes one with justice.

WHAM!

"No way!" Courageously, Amoy carefully invites the cooks to come near, and soon, others gather closely, abandoning their tables and hot meals to witness the show. Thus, boosting morale and excitement throughout the eatery. Destin, however, has reflections of his own.

"Arghh!" Arresting him by the sleeve of his heavy weather coat, a single gold tooth quietly falls through his cracked lips. "A fucking cop?" he reveals. Bobbi's badge slips out from her jacket, exposed for all to see.

"Pimp in distress?" she mocks. "Kicking your ass is going to bring me so much satisfaction." Mounting him like a helpless trick, she begins to thrash him, pounding on his face with her gloved knuckles.

"Yeah! Beat his ass!"

WHAM! WHAM! WHAM!

DING!

SOME STRIPPER BITCH

"Drop the knife, **Percy**."

Many offenders have witnessed the barrel of **Sally Mae**, gluing their blameworthy acts and following arrests to the weapon's serial number, and as for Bobbi, she is her handler. "I can do this all night." Her powerful .38 Special snub nose revolver does just that, raising fear and reassurance throughout the diner.

"Easy, Bobbi! I ain't mean no harm, baby!" Releasing the switchblade, Percy, dead to his rights, immediately surrenders to Sally Mae, Bobbi, and her badge. To a significant capacity, fancy men are relatively common in Freeland. However, Percy has managed to slip through the long arm of the law more times than most.

"Geez, Bobbi, can we just eat already?" Destin suggests. Glimpsing at the girls seeking her for assurance, Bobbi finally accepts her surroundings and lowers her firearm.

"Sure, let's eat."

AMBROSIA: SEASON ONE

#

Surrounded by housing criminals and more, the Fastback sits idle under a familiar street sign. The vehicle's cloudy exhaust ascends through the splitting cold to reveal Wailing Ninya Place. Meanwhile, Bobbi, turning a blind eye to it all, endures the massacre that happened Thanksgiving morning.

It's only been an hour, and after hearing the daunting report from the Pathologist, she senses defeat, trapped with new explicit thoughts.

"Talk to me, Blake." Forensics had combed the area, and The Blue released the scene back to the public, who have moved on. But how can she forget this very spot in the street? It's where her sister took her last breath, and now, there are no more traces of Blake.

Looming over the gas pedal, Bobbi prepares to leave the stage when two locals

SOME STRIPPER BITCH

approach her position from behind the right-hand side. Risk at this hour is standard, nudging her to embrace Sally Mae for safe measure. Exposed in her side mirror, the Detective counts two worn city dwellers concealed behind the hoods of their large fabrics and loose blue jeans.

Gripping her weapon tightly as they drag near, she finally exhales and stands down.

"Man, what doesn't go on around here? Remember that body on Turkey Day?" Bobbi overhears.

"Yeah, some stripper bitch, right? Caught out in the cold, if you know what I mean. But someone must have seen something." Bobbi takes notice.

"It's a damn shame."

Studying the brick towers of Freeland Public Housing, she searches seven stories upward to find movement from a window of Building #19.

"I hear you, little sister."

GIBSON PRIME PRECINCT

75th

Date: September 01, 1976

At the start, I told Bobbi that being a policewoman was risky; I wrote her off. Nonetheless, she persevered through all obstacles, and to my surprise, she didn't fold. She fought tooth and nail for that damn promotion, too, and as far as I'm concerned, she still has no idea how to police.

Now, standing on over twenty-six closed cases solved in three weeks, including a major bust that led me to fourteen essential arrests, she has proven to stand on her own, which I cannot contend.

She arrived in that Fastback just under three months ago. I don't like her, and neither do my boys, but if the Lieutenant swears by her, then so do I.

Sergeant Howie Liveright

RIVERWALK PURGATORY

RIVERWALK PURGATORY

CENTRAL FREELAND
METRO NORTH RIVERWALK
00:00 AM

"This shit better not crack!"

Discovered along an icy stretch, Bobbi stumbles and slides, and as for the fortified ridged channels of her combat boots, they fail to grip a frozen river beneath her.

Surrounded by grass terraces, a glorified sundeck, and a magnificent view stretching to East Freeland's skyline, Metro North's prime waterfront replaces industry with recreation as one of the city's most scenic inspirations.

"Don't worry, Bobbi, it's only ice." Bobbi whips around. However, to her surprise, no one is near, and yet, her voice—

"Why do you choose the worst games to play, Blake." Its forty-five-mile carriage road passes by a heartwarming music hall that has attracted the two since they were little.

AMBROSIA: SEASON ONE

"Hurry, Bobbi; they're about to begin" Then, the policewoman, alerted, shifts to witness statues of her allies encircling her, judging her, and as they materialize before her, she jolts back, nearly losing her step. Yet, beyond the shock and fright, Bobbi is watchful, but still, no sign of Blake. *"C'mon, Bobbi!"*

"Blake—where are you?" Suddenly, her sister's child-like soul dashes ahead. "Blake!" she shouts. Then, as instinct and adrenaline collide within, she breaks through, only to be confronted by Officer Liveright in his dying form.

"Aren't you out of your jurisdiction, Bobbi?" She's dealt with his kind on plenty of occasions. Hence, she shoves her way through him, ditching his body to crumble and wither away, "Hurry up, will ya! I ain't got all day…"

"Blake—BLAKE!" Bobbi cries; she is exhausted. "How could I lose her again?" Meanwhile, a sudden flash emits from a distance, following the intrusive existence of

RIVERWALK PURGATORY

Lieutenant Schillaci commanding a fierce
ice storm dangerous enough to threaten the
frozen river she stands on.

"Dammit, Howard, those girls are lost—
Blake is lost! Haven't you learned that yet?"
His words are harsh as the icy wind blows,
"How bad do you want this case?" he adds.

His laughter taunts the brave Detective.
Nonetheless, Bobbi must try, even if she must
go against her moral judgments and even—
KNOCK, KNOCK!

KNOCK, KNOCK!

KNOCK, KNOCK!

FREELAND PUBLIC HOUSING COMPLEX
SECOND FLOOR - BUILDING #19
08:03 AM

KNOCK, KNOCK, KNOCK!

The petite knuckle pounding at the door comes to a rest at **7F** to expose none other than Bobbi, awaiting with her shield dangling out in the open.

Eager for a witness, she fastens her fists, wrenching at the leather every three seconds. Moments in, she takes notice of the stained wallpaper peeling away from the edges above the chipped apartment door. The hallway is vacant, filthy, and reeks of urine. Eyeing her exits, she chose to come by early to avoid unwanted attention from the projects.

KNOCK, KNOCK!

Time is dwindling. If she doesn't gain a response quickly, the residents will fill the narrow hallways in no time. Thus, trouble will follow.

KNOCK, KNOCK, KNOCK!

It's also possible that even a trained eye couldn't acquire a worthy description if it weren't for the neighboring kids kicking out the street lamps in the courtyard. Nonetheless, someone is behind the door, and she is not giving up on her first possible lead.

"What do you want?"

Eventually, a gravelly voice slips between the door's edge and affixed chain lock to uncover a sadly hunched-over tenant wearing a fair nightgown and her hair in rollers staring through her, figuratively speaking. Sensing uneasiness, Bobbi identifies herself and moves to make her badge known.

"Hello, I am Detective Howard from Gibson Prime Precinct. May I…" Yet, as experienced as one's introduction can be, Bobbi couldn't avoid the elder woman's endless gaze. Thus, indicating something

KNOCK, KNOCK!

peculiar. Nonetheless, Bobbi, with bravery, continues, "I'm continuing the investigation of the dancer murdered outside your building just the past holiday. Can I ask you a couple of questions?" Seeking confirmation, she aims for easy words to gain the tenant's trust across the board.

Examining the policewoman with high suspicion, she notes Bobbi's boots, her leather jacket and badge, and finally, the Detective's face.

"You look like *her*," she whispers. Stunned, Bobbi can't explain the feeling washing over her, but it's somewhat familiar. However, the tenant offers no sign of letting Bobbi into her home.

"I'm sorry...*her*?" she beckons. Is she referring to Blake? Bobbi's pulse quickens at the idea. Thus, suspense rises all the same.

"That poor soul...she didn't deserve that. None of them did," she utters.

AMBROSIA: SEASON ONE

Next, a sudden pang shimmers down the Detective's neck from a strange sensation prompting her to act.

"Beyond your window," Bobbi implies, "What did you see out there?" Nudging her boot discreetly under their noses, she inches her way beneath the tenant for the particulars. "Perhaps someone from the area, someone familiar maybe?" she invites.

"They're all in trouble, detective," she overshares. Next, her doubtful eyebrows gradually indicate a struggle behind her perceptual-motor abilities before staring back into nothingness.

"Ma'am?" She barely said a word after that, and as for the Detective, time was nearly at its closing. "Perhaps someone who lives with you witnessed something that morning?" Unfortunately for Bobbi, her questions fail to stick to the landing. The older woman's expression grew thin, and alas, her distrust returned.

KNOCK, KNOCK!

"Who are you? What do you want?"

Her times up. Tucking her badge, Bobbi shifts her focus and starts towards the exit. It's as if someone had written all her information on a big blackboard, taken an eraser, and wiped it all away. Meanwhile, the now grief-stricken woman invites others to observe the fleeing Detective, drawing unwanted eyes to the ongoing crisis. "They're not safe at Diamonds!"

ARE YOU AWAKE?

ARE YOU AWAKE?

**OLD FREELAND
SUNNYSIDE HEIGHTS
11:48 PM**

"Bobbi?"

The heat from an iron radiator underneath a frosty window encircles the room while two girls huddle closely under a wool blanket. Around this time of the year, they share a bed due to the drastic temperature dropping all throughout Freeland. Yet, they didn't mind. They preferred sleeping together anyway, being best friends as well as siblings.

Tossing with trouble, the youngest turns towards the older and utters this to say:

"Pst, Bobbi?"

"What is it now, Blake?" Lacking empathy, Bobbi shuffles with her back turned, inciting Blake to pursue an innocent exchange.

"Are you asleep?"

"No, but I'd like to be, stupid." Her harsh response only illustrates that the two have a

AMBROSIA: SEASON ONE

warm bond.

"Okay, just making sure," she ends, cuddling softly behind her sister. Her tiny voice trails off, begging Bobbi to revisit her last comment.

"What's on your mind?" she asks. Bobbi can feel sleep calling to her. Nonetheless, for the sake of her baby sister, she attempts to keep an ear out.

"You know how it always takes you a long time to jump in the rope—"

"Are you serious?" Bobbi snaps. "Why are you talking about double-dutch at this time of night?" However, the question finally registers, and undoubtedly, she leaves her drowsiness behind.

"I think I know why."

Now sitting on the bed, Blake pulls the thick comforter around her body and invites Bobbi to join her as they both face off in the darkness. "I've been watching you…" Blake reveals, "All I'm saying is you take too long to

ARE YOU AWAKE?

jump in the rope 'cause you doubt yourself, like, every time." Sunk in concern, Bobbi tugs on the blanket they share to cover her worries while deeply considering what her sister is conveying.

"I wasn't there to save you, little sister."

"It's okay. Besides, there's still time to find my killer. You're just scared, afraid of what will happen when you do." Shaken with what appears to be the truth, Bobbi latches onto Blake and pulls her in when suddenly, a warm substance forms underneath them, reeking of iron.

"B-Blake?"

CONNECTING THE DOTS

CONNECTING THE DOTS

SOUTH FREELAND
CROWN HEIGHTS TERRACE
11:48 PM

TAP! TAP! TAP!

Responding like a firecracker, Detective Howard jolts toward the dashboard while her heart races. Meantime, her hand hovers softly over her firearm resting near her hip.

"Step away from my vehicle!" she announces. The frigid cold had crept through the Mustang's heavy metal shell, evoking goose bumps to rise under her jacket.

"Roll down your window." Scanning the stranger beyond her frosty window, she manages to make out his frame, skin color, and arm resting atop her Fastback's hood. Yet, remembering Blake's death and her passion for solving it, she exhales softly, relaxes her weapon, and goes for the door panel.

"Hang on!" she shouts. Why am I doing this…she imagines, and as prospect

AMBROSIA: SEASON ONE

meets fortune, she releases the window to find him making curious with her.

"You a'ight?" Filled with desire are his eyes and his voice, very deep. Revealing his neat teeth with a swipe of his tongue, the stranger begins to stack up. At a peek, the eager man's hands are considerable, wide enough to reach her lips, curvy parts, and perhaps, her soul. His brown skin, ivory teeth, and beard are framed well, and as for his delivery, he is tempting.

"I'm fine…just waiting for a friend."

"At this hour?" Surrendering to his player practice, she smiles, and her eyes follow. Feigning ignorance, however, it's ridiculous for anyone in their right mind to be sound asleep in a forsaken parking lot smack dab in South Freeland's midpoint. "You don't look like you from around here," he says. Yet aware, Bobbi seeks the advantage to eliminate any threat and summons him for approval of attraction.

CONNECTING THE DOTS

"Step back so I can see you," she incites while laying her eyes upon him. Telling by a shy grin, he yields to her and seeks a wide stance just under a street lamp, and alas, Bobbi can now rest her eyes on a much broader view of him. "Stand right there." He is what women would have described as a black God. His lengthy locks hang loose like long dark ropes sprouting from his dome, bearing strength and health as they sway with his movements.

He's dressed well for a man wandering the vacant lot. On his left wrist, a custom twenty-carat diamond steel Rolex catches her eye, while a stunning ring filled with stones rests on his right finger.

"You like what you see?" he teases. Most women are interested in men draped in fine jewelry, but not Bobbi; her type wouldn't be seen at this hour of the night. But something about him,

"I do." She's shocked. Hearing her tongue loosen to match him feels different, and even

AMBROSIA: SEASON ONE

better, it feels good.

#

"WUH-HACK!"

Laboring beyond an ongoing exchange behind his door ajar, Lieutenant Schillaci fails to contain a nasty cough and goes to wash it down with a closed fist full of whiskey.

"Damn, Jon Claire, you don't sound good." Having been blasted with the department's daily reports, he fails to mention the sensitive case he foolishly surrendered to Bobbi.

"Shove it, Liveright." Thanksgiving's crime scene has yet to be forgotten and so, the Lieutenant pours himself another glass.

"Jon, the cold isn't kind after midnight." Sitting across from him, a familiar policeman working the morning of Blake's murder endures his Lieutenant's distressing wheeze and rattle.

CONNECTING THE DOTS

"WUH-HACK! Shut it—I'm trying to process this mess." Frustration finds Schillaci in the presence of Liveright, for the two have pending matters to sort out. Then, nearing Schillaci's ward, a slender silhouette pokes Jon's attention while he snuffs Liveright's welfare. "Ah, Burkman!"

Reporting after a brutal seventeen-hour shift, Destin stops at the door to find Liveright reclining on the ward's couch. Having differences yet to be dismissed between them, the bitter police officer peacefully places his cap on the open space next to him. Seeing this, he immediately chooses the path of least resistance and acknowledges their discussion.

"Need me to come back, Lieutenant?"

"What I need is a good explanation," Jon responds, "What were you and Howard doing damn-near outside jurisdiction?"

"Nothing to explain, sir." Glancing at Liveright, Destin takes a stand against the unnecessary matter, seeks an opportunity

AMBROSIA: SEASON ONE

to characterize his role in his precinct, and pushes the envelope further, "Is there something against the policy to dine with co-workers, Lieutenant?"

"I don't give a shit who you eat with, and even funnier, who you eat, Burkman."

"That's right, Jon does the feeding around here, Destin." Liveright's tongue slips out. Yet, the Pathologist fails to budge at the bitter policeman's inferior comment.

"Percy would have hurt that girl, and Howard happened to be in the area to stop him, sir," Destin claims. He believes Bobbi and isn't prepared to let her down after all she has, tolerated and endured.

"Cut the bull, Burkman. You know better than to discuss open cases outside my walls, and unless you have a private account to share with me, you can tell Howard the cold outside will be more welcoming than my own hands, is that understood?"

At this moment, Jon's dominance proves

CONNECTING THE DOTS

that Burkman has fallen into the lion's den, and the Lieutenant of the Town is starving.

#

Later, at the vacant lot, the two have been conversing, sharing stories, and smiles with modest applied contact; they've found common ground.

"So, you dance here?" says the stranger, who finds himself leaning on her car at the driver's side. His charisma is, at best, contagious, and as for Bobbi,

"I—" Charmed entirely; perhaps she has shared more than she should have allowed, as her graceless silence following suggests so.

"Listen, I have to run—see you around." With little time only allowed by chance, they've formed more than interest, and Bobbi, worshiping him from a distance, is inclined to learn more. The stranger may be involved in

AMBROSIA: SEASON ONE

the usual dealings, pushing smack and roughing guys up.

"And you are?" Strolling in the direction of the brilliant building traced in glowing colored rays, the man of mystery arrests his footing and responds,

"Come find out."

COME FIND OUT

AMBROSIA: SEASON ONE

DIAMOND'S GENTLEMEN'S CLUB
MONEY NIGHT
12:01 AM

"Yo! There's a line!"

Ignoring the streak of men varying in age, status, and desires, the stranger in passing holds his words until he nears the magnific entrance to Diamond's hand-crafted in fine timber enhanced with dazzling crystal rimming its ends.

"**Sharif**, come to play?" Standing before him are the doorkeepers, tough enough, and armed enough, to stop those who may dare to violate the nightclub's entry code. However, if there's anyone with equal street credit who has never given them problems on any visit is *him*.

"Nah, none of that, fellas." These guys, voices baritone and brutish, are giants. Where did they find monsters like them anyways? The damaged skin forged over their knuckles

COME FIND OUT

appears as rough as leather, and their faces; don't even bother. "How much can you three hold?" Revealing a heap of bills from his coat pocket, he offers a bold stance unburdened by war. He cannot afford any trouble tonight, but do they know this?

"How much you got?" one responds, signaling the others to frisk him. "Any weapons on you, Sharif?" The felon's eyes communicate concern, and yet, he chooses silence.

Once verified with a loose pat-down, they accept his generosity and grant him access beyond the threshold of the scandalous gentlemen's club.

"Signal me if they pull up," he warns.

Dodging the lights before the ultimate showcase, Sharif obeys the shadows that lure Freeland's honest workers, husbands, and, of course, the hustlers to indulge. Nonetheless, this is his scene, and the scene owes him acceptance.

Inches away from a large arrangement of

AMBROSIA: SEASON ONE

black velvet curtains, he prepares his hands and carefully parts them to expose the main floor shrouded in sex, sin, and where money unlocks fantasies. Joining the precarious set, strobes of lustrous hues gliding above him beat his jewelry, from the diamonds in his ears to the rocks in his ring, initiating him to pass.

The racy atmosphere welcomes him, luring him deep down with floating cash bills, evocative music, and captivating bare women dancing on multiple platforms. Women of all colors are found here, and only in South Freeland can they promise a payout that even the local banks can't compete, and while many men imagine Diamond's a secret palace of loose women, others hail it the trap. In fact, they build establishments like this for guys like him: treacherous, heartless, and other pictures imagined in the mind that can define a street felon like Sharif.

Exploring the set with his weapon tucked

COME FIND OUT

along his waistband, the erotic entertainers immediately identify him, placing their deceptive eyes upon his diamond carat count; he is a destructive man, and *they* like that. Furthermore, his reputation has an unformidable reach, so when he's around, it's a subtle sign for the girls to keep their shit in check.

The felon resumes his path leaving the aura of lust behind him to access a spiraling staircase leading to a dark exodus whom some have anointed Eden.

#

Snow crystals fall over Freeland and the Pathologist, well-clothed for the weather, stepping off bus **#29** at South Town Station. Shuffling past a popular newspaper rack, he tucks his face to avoid the dead dancer's published article on the front page.

Crossing a familiar street and into a community asleep, the modest workman hikes a

AMBROSIA: SEASON ONE

powdered path leading to an empty block. He knows this walk. His brisk pace and mindful steps indicate that he treads this route weekly, yet he is tenser than ever. Hence, bringing random bouts of exhaustion.

Reaching the stoop, Destin stops to gather himself before keying the door to his home. He wouldn't dare. Yet, a daring career man can only hope his dangerous work won't creep into his private life. However, standing in front of his peaceful home, vivid snapshots of the spellbinding, blonde-haired Detective keeps his mind and, perhaps, his heart.

Entering a generous space, framed photographs of his dutiful son and his many accomplishments grace the entrance to the family room. His career has earned him a legacy, but his great responsibility to aid his city has kept him from attending his child's precious triumphs on several occasions.

"Your father's home." he pleads in silence. Meanwhile, his other half rests just upstairs.

COME FIND OUT

Switching his briefcase from one hand to the other, he seizes the cold railing while climbing the warm steps leading to his wife, as represented in many portraits of him and her.

"I wonder where you are, Bobbi."

Attempting to suck in another breath, Destin aspires to bury his sentiments for the other woman on his way up.

#

LIVE / NUDE / INSIDE

Eyeing the fancy cars, expanding sections of men, and their mannish banter growing by the minute outside the intensifying structure, Bobbi's adrenaline races as she plants her combat boot on the gravel with a leather duffle bag carried over her shoulder.

Recapping the events that sparked this investigation, from Blake's body found at Wailing Ninya Place to the tenant of room 7F,

AMBROSIA: SEASON ONE

she is firm in her choice, and nothing shall stop her.

"I'm sure I'll find answers here, even if I have to beat it out of them." Thinking back to her unsettling encounter with Jon, he failed to give her explicit directives, and now, she is about to enter Diamond's, where her sister had last danced before she was—

POP!

The Detective immediately registers the turn of events and drops her duffle bag to retrieve her revolver.

POP—POP—POP!

Bobbi sprints towards what has become pandemonium. The active-shooter has yet to be seen, and as madness rises, she fights through with the infamous gentlemen's club in her sight.

TO BE CONTINUED...

BECOMING WANTED

AMBROSIA: SEASON ONE

Meeting David was a great experience; he is unique, and when I discovered his narratives captured through photography, I instantly became excited and prepared to dive in.

Over the years, the two of us grew very close, and when we landed *Ambrosia*, I knew it would be unlike any other story I'd seen.

Becoming Bobbi brings out my alter ego. She's witty, sassy, and pushy sometimes but all around: she is 100% badass!

Likewise, I can especially relate to her because I once was a dancer. So it's easy to bring out the hardcore and sexiness my character requires.

It's been a pleasure working with Become Wanted Entertainment, and I hope to see her in theaters soon; and how she's performing so far, I believe there will be more to come.

Teamwork made this dream work!
Tajai, the HBIC

STINGER

AMBROSIA: SEASON ONE

LOWER FREELAND
LUCKY'S CAFÉ
3:00 AM

Arctic winds whip unmercifully outside **Lucky's**, a dismal diner in Freeland's filthiest domain north of Gibson Prime.

Lower Avenue was once filled with vitality, drawing commercial support from nearby districts. Now, rats are free to roam the gutters, where even the homeless are too afraid to dwell near. But is it the vermin that lost fear, or is it *him*?

Entering the ruined restaurant, Sharif bypasses two unfriendly guardians, tailored in all-black, who appear to have been expecting him. In contrast, these guys are built like no other. Their fists are fatty, their eyes are tight and beady, and their skin is feverishly red, like the commonly known coffee berry.

"Merry Christmas, you filthy animals." Greeting tough guys always bear trouble, but

STINGER

as tension climbs, his words discover their cold ears, for he knows: they are forbidden to speak with him.

Opening the doors to the dining theater, a broad silhouette of a wide man, traced beneath the moonlight casting from the restaurant's upper expanse window, can be seen feasting when suddenly, a bottomless voice pierces the silence, startling Sharif where he stands.

"Come here, Sharif; I have something to tell you."

Trembling not from the cold temperature, the outsider steps onward where he is beckoned, passing several dining sections provided white round runners, milky-bone china, and silken threads of a spiderweb accumulated throughout a lack of business.

From the doors, the space holds a rank smell. But, if Sharif were to describe it, he would say it was a smell of decay. An odor he knows all too well.

AMBROSIA: SEASON ONE

Reaching the elegant's section, he finally acknowledges the shadowy character dining across from his most-treasured guest, encased delicately in a dainty photo skeleton resting on a swirly iron easel.

"Dorian," he greets. Searching for a seat nearby, "Can I pull up a chair?"

"Stand." The gray man's voice spares no compassion for him. "I like you, Sharif." Exposing his hand for a swallow of wine, Dorian worships diamonds, but unlike those entrenched in Sharif's jewelry, his stones are embedded in his flesh. "Now that I can see your face tell me, what was your involvement?" His English could be better. However, how he speaks is good enough for many others governed under his law.

"They were meant for me," Sharif confesses. Then, rising from the round table, the gray man's dark despair shifts, becoming wider and wider, consuming everything in the room. Never the one to cower, he grows

STINGER

rigid in the sight of Dorian's beady black eyes while inching for his pistol with the ends of his fingertips.

"And, what about you, Lieutenant?" Entering from Sharif's left, Schillaci appears, leading with gleaming silver bars pinned to the collar tips of his down-duty union shirt.

"Oh, me?" Inhaling intensely with spite rooted in his eyes, the Lieutenant bends to share his most recent affair at the nightspot with the gray man. "Last time I checked, the girls were great, and Diamond's was in good order," he brags.

"What kind of mess have you with the Haitians?" Knowing of every illicit party functioning in East, West and South Freeland, Dorian's suspicion is warranted, and yet—

"The Jamaicans," Sharif asserts, "And yeah...I'll fix it," he assures to then seek a rather nasty comeback for his rival, Schillaci, to bite on, "And our Lieutenant here will make sure that arrests are made too. Isn't that right,

AMBROSIA: SEASON ONE

Jon?" Perhaps, Schillaci underestimates him; after all, there is no honor among thieves.

"Keep talking, asshole! WUH-HACK!" Balling up in pain, the policeman, lacking discourse, eventually regains his position to find embarrassment while Dorian waits, "I'll see what I can do."

"So be it." Lastly, Sharif pulls away from the table, eyeing the burning exit sign ahead, "Do I have anything else to worry about?"

"Nah."

Avoiding Dorian's wicked snare, he can still feel the gray man's eyes darting at him, and while his weapon remains secured along his front just behind his coat, he would be wise to carry on, for he is outnumbered by two and possibly, outgunned by one.

The two have a problematic relationship. On the one hand, Dorian appears to favor Sharif, and on the other, Jon has committed enough forbidden acts for one to bypass the burden he has carried over the years.

STINGER

"That's it? He walks?" Suddenly, Jon yanks on his left sleeve to reveal his prosthetic device, and while his temper spills over, a hand cannon implanted in the base of his palm drives through cybernetically. "Dorian!" The policeman has earned the gray man's ears, "I want this guy out of my way!"

"Sharif!" The giant's voice splits the darkness, stopping Sharif from exiting. Merely steps away, he gradually becomes utterly mortified, stunned at the sight of Dorian's infected skin and raw diamonds protruding from his face.

"Yah?" Unexpectedly, Sharif's loyal roots slip through his teeth to further anger the hideous man.

"Diamond's, and everything associated with it *will* be mine…don't you forget that, ***Outsider***."

#

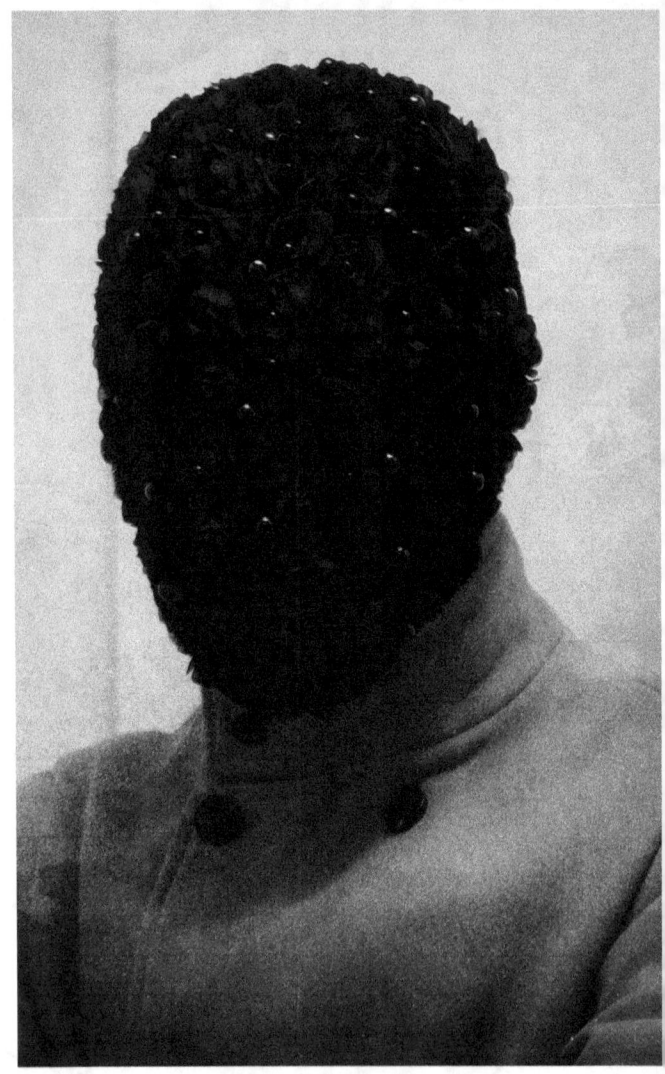

GIBSON PRIME PRECINCT

75th

Date: November 22, 1976

    No one knows his real name, yet his legacy is widely understood. In Freeland, mobsters have been printed, killers have been captured, and convicts have a special place behind bars. However, this man, whoever he is, evades capture not by his uncanny abilities but because to summon him is actual suicide.

    I don't have much to report on this one, and it's safe to keep it that way. Besides, those curious about finding him didn't return, and I'm open to expressing how uninterested I am in how or why.

    So, in short: don't pursue him, stay away from his bloody mess, and don't dare speak his name.

Sergeant Howie Liveright

AMBROSIA: SEASON ONE

Strutting down **Brooke Ave**, an enticing woman, dressed rather suggestive, hurries to beat the chilling cold and, perhaps, something else. Draped in mink, dazzling gems, and a flashy clutch bag crammed with dollar bills, she is also clasping equalizing protection tucked along her backside.

Her path chosen isn't one she hasn't undergone before. It's a familiar street where another woman in her profession was found killed weeks before Blake.

Dodging hissing steam rising from the gutter, the woman is watchful. Meanwhile, her instincts beg her to reach for the small pistol, and as wickedness falls, she snaps.

"Who's there?" She can't make out anything beyond her wrists, scarlet red coated fingernails, and chrome weapon raised; fear is near. Aside from the flickering street lamp and a ghostly breeze escaping the alley ahead, someone watching haunts the woman in heels. "Who's there, dammit?"

STINGER

Suddenly, wide dingy headlights from an aged sedan fix her in the center of the street, revealing her tall stature and full spiced flowing hair, curvy hips, and lengthy legs squeezed in tall boots. Fear has arrived.

The car's warm rays are too bright for her eyes. Thus, she lowers her aim, stumbles back, and sadly loses her step, allowing fear to take over.

*"Are you afraid, **Joanna**?"*

Gripping the driver's side door, a slender character wearing a long coat emerges from the vehicle and begins to approach her, stirring panic along the way.

Collapsed without her firearm, Joanna's eyes are drawn to his hideous mask, stitched and twisted with unbelievable materials unfamiliar to the average eye. His clothing articles are unrecognizable due to the intense backlight beaming from his car. Furthermore, his hollow voice and overall stance are bizarre, conveying killer without a doubt.

AMBROSIA: SEASON ONE

"Fuck you!" she shouts. Then, with a bold flick of her working switchblade—

SHINK!

"Ah...another brave dancer doomed." Misfortune and unbelief have fallen upon Joanna, and no matter where she turns, even she begins to believe that there is no escape.

"Who are you?" Finally, fear has conquered her, her knife will fail her, and where tears form to fall, his terrifying eyes have taken notice.

"I am Freeland's nightmare, and you will not survive this night, darling."

www.becomewanted.com

www.ingramcontent.com/pod-product-compliance
Lightning Source LLC
LaVergne TN
LVHW021952060526
838201LV00049B/1680